FINN MacCOUL

and His Fearless Wife

Hodder
Children's
Books

a division of Hodder Headline Limited

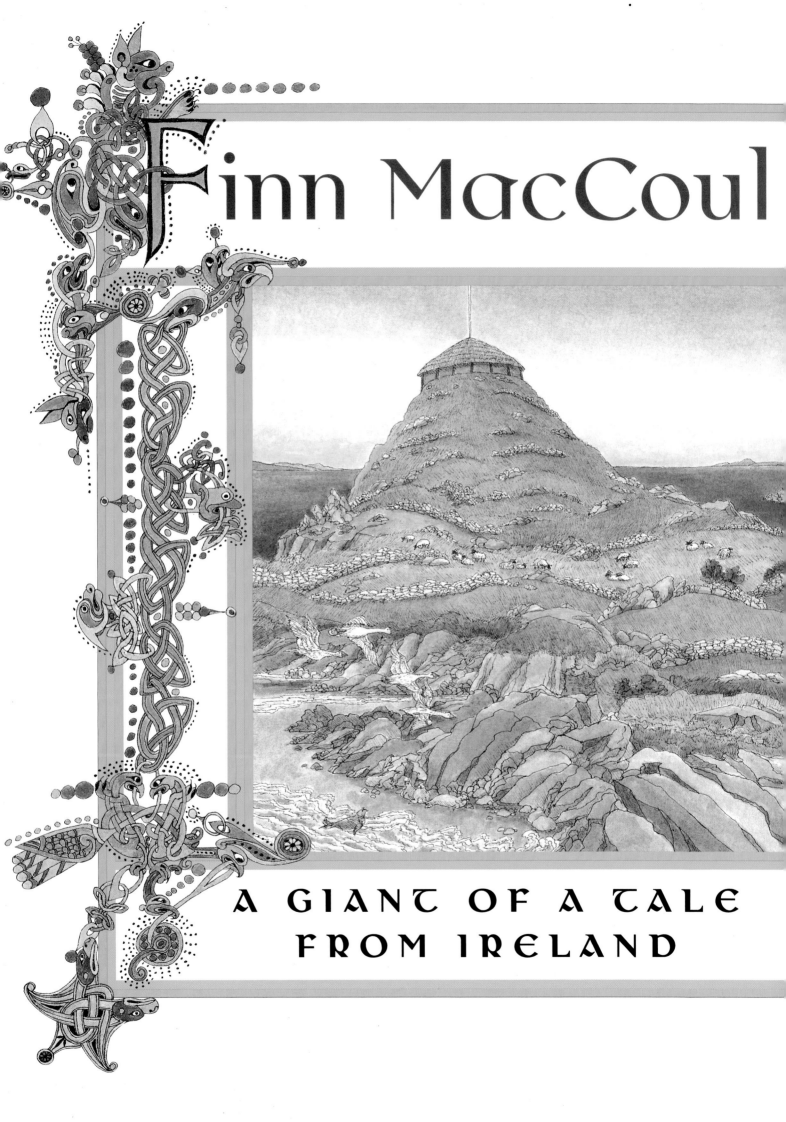

Finn MacCoul

A GIANT OF A TALE
FROM IRELAND

and His Fearless Wife

RETOLD AND ILLUSTRATED BY Robert Byrd

First published in 1999 by Dutton Children's Books
A division of Penguin Putnam Books for Young Readers
345 Hudson Street
New York, New York 10014

First published in Great Britain in 1999
by Macdonald Young Books
an imprint of Wayland Publishers Ltd

This edition published in 2004 by
Hodder Children's Books
A division of Hodder Headline Limited
338 Euston Road, London, NW1 3BH

A catalogue record for this book
is available from the British Library

Printed in China by WKT Company Ltd

ISBN 0 340 90286 8

Ah, faeries, dancing under the moon,
A Druid land, a Druid tune!
—W. B. Yeats

For my wife, Ginger,
and for all those who have known,
or will yet know, the realm of Faery

And who has not heard of the mighty Finn MacCoul, the most famous of the Irish giants who lived back in the days when the great High Kings ruled that fair Emerald Isle?

When Finn was born, his gran took him and reared him in a great oak tree. She feared for his life, you see, because the king was so jealous of the child's size and strength. Even as a mere babe, Finn was already famous. It was said he ate one hundred potatoes and thirty cabbages on his first birthday, and two hundred potatoes and sixty cabbages on his second. He drank so much milk that twelve cows had to follow him wherever he played.

When Finn grew to be a young man, his gran took him further into the deep oak forest. There she bid him farewell.

"Ah, my fine Finn," she said, "'tis time it is, lad, that you find the secrets of knowing and truth. Follow the River Boyne till you reach the faeries who guard the mysteries of the ancient ways of the world."

When Finn arrived, the High King of the Faeries welcomed him. "Great size you may have now, but when you are a man, you will need wisdom and courage besides. You must eat from Fintan, the Salmon of Knowledge."

On the night of the high summer moon, the faeries caught the salmon with a golden net. The king gave Fintan to Finn, who cooked and ate the magic fish, but in so doing, he burned his thumb.

As Finn sucked his thumb to ease the pain, the salmon magically reappeared again in the pool and spoke:

> *Finn, 'tis knowledge and wisdom I give to you.*
> *A great leader you'll be before you are through –*
> *Just let your thumb show you a fair trick or two.*
> *Be loyal and honest and seek your own way,*
> *And a woman's wit and courage will win you the day!*

The salmon bowed deeply and jumped back into the water.

From that day forward, whenever Finn needed to see into the future, he simply sucked his thumb.

ventually Finn did grow taller than any man in Ireland and became Chieftain of the Fianna, as true as it was told. Now, about this time it was, he and his men decided to build a great stone bridge between Ireland and Scotland. Half the men pulled great rocks out of the earth and threw them miles out to sea. The other half, riding on great whales, caught the boulders and stacked them one on top of the next.

Finn planned to name this bridge the Giant's Causeway – him-self, of course.

But as they drew closer and closer to Scotland, Finn began to make out the figure of a man, standing on the distant shore. A giant of a man.

When naught but half a league separated the end of the stone bridge from the land, Finn at last could clearly see the fearsome fellow waiting at the ready, glaring across the surf.

"Tell me, my good man," the stranger roared, with a mighty voice that caused a small tidal wave, "if you finish this bridge, and I follow it, will it lead me to Finn MacCoul?"

"And what business might you have with Finn MacCoul?" answered Finn, shaking in his shoes.

"Aren't we the nosy one?" the stranger taunted. "And just who might you be, you blockhead?"

"I am just a poor cowherd," answered Finn. "But I work for Finn MacCoul. Away he is now, and no one'll be knowing for sure when he's to return."

"And how big a man is this Finn MacCoul?" asked the stranger.

"Ah, Finn would be twice your size now," replied Finn nervously.

"Humph," muttered the stranger. "Well, when you yourself see him, tell him Cucullin will be paying him a call!" And so saying, he strode off down the beach.

Cucullin! Finn knew the name and shivered down to the very soles of his feet, he did. Cucullin was another giant whose fame spread far and wide. He had roamed the countryside for nigh on a hundred years, swearing never to rest, day or night, come rain or snow, until he had bested every man alive in a true test of strength. It was said that this Cucullin was so strong that when he stomped his foot, the whole earth shook. It also was said that he had once flattened a lightning bolt with a single blow of his fist.

Finn knew he had to keep out of Cucullin's way. So with a pine tree for a walking stick, and his faithful hound Bran running at his side, he made for home as fast as he could. Now, Finn had the good fortune of living at the very tip-top of Knockmany Hill. When asked why he lived in such a high and windy place, Finn always said it was because he loved the feeling of a breeze in his face and the clouds in his hair.

But if the truth be known, the real reason Finn lived on the tip-top of Knockmany Hill was so that he could look out for other giants who might come to challenge him – especially Cucullin.

When Finn arrived home, his lovely wife, Oonagh, paused in her work and looked down at him. "Why, husband," she called out, "whatever is it that brings you home at this time of day?"

"Why, the lovely sight of yourself," replied Finn, quite out of breath.

"Hmmm," said Oonagh. "I don't believe it, but come inside, and I'll fix you some food and drink."

"Oonagh, my dearest," said Finn, " 'tis true! I was lonely for your sweet face, and I missed you sure as the flowers miss the rain, and—"

"Finn MacCoul!" interrupted Oonagh. "Enough of this nonsense now. And don't you be trying any of your foolishness with me – for after all, who in all the world knows you better than I? Pray man, tell me what your trouble might be."

Finn gave a deep sigh. "Oonagh, my love, Cucullin is coming; I know it." Finn sucked for a moment on his great thumb. "Sure it's true, he will be here at dawn, the beast! When he stomps his foot, the earth shakes. And he carries a flattened bolt of lightning in his pocket. If I run from him, I am a coward – yet if I stay, he will squash me like a bug! Can you do nothing for me, woman?"

"Easy now, Finn, and don't you be so gloomy," said Oonagh thoughtfully. "Leave him to me, and do exactly as I say."

ow if truth be told, Oonagh did not yet know what to do. But as a child, you see, she also had been taught the old secrets of magic by the faeries. It was said, in fact, that Oonagh's black cat Ròsdubh was a faery herself. Because of Oonagh's noble spirit and courage, she had been trusted with the safekeeping of the Sacred Faery Harp.

This harp hung on a diamond nail on the wall. When Oonagh took it down and touched its golden strings, the ancient faery voices rhymed her a riddle, singing like tiny silver bells:

Oonagh, fearless wife of Finn,
Say nothing rash; do nothing wild.
Think breads and threads both thick and thin;
Nine colours bright tie man to child.

Oonagh then knew exactly what to do. She took nine woollen threads of different colours and wove them into three braids. One braid she put on her right arm, another she tied at her heart, and the third around her left ankle.

And then she danced to the magic voices, spinning round and round and round. She knew now that she could not fail.

Oonagh worked all through the night. First she made twenty-one great loaves of bread, putting a great iron pot inside each loaf and baking them all in a great clay oven. These she piled next to some ordinary loaves of bread.

Next she took a great pail of milk and made twenty-one great rounds of cheese. These she put with a pile of large yellow stones.

At the break of dawn, she leaned out the door and gave three loud whistles.

This was the old way the Irish let strangers know they were welcome. When Cucullin heard the three whistles, he began to climb up Knockmany Hill.

Oonagh dragged out a big cradle and said, "Be quick, now, Finn, hop in. Cover up and lie snug, saying not a word — not a peep out of you, now! Just leave this business to me."

No sooner had Finn squeezed himself into the cradle than the house began to shake with every mighty step Cucullin took. As Cucullin pounded on the door, Finn burrowed under the covers and moaned.

"Be still, man," whispered Oonagh, "and just you remember this: All of Cucullin's strength is to be found in the gold finger of his left hand."

Cucullin could barely fit through the door, but he came in shouting, "And where is the coward Finn MacCoul?"

"Why, he left the house in a rage, didn't he," replied Oonagh calmly. "For it seems that some buffoon of a giant named Cucullin was at the causeway looking for him, and Finn went to try and catch him, he did. For the poor giant's sake, I hope they don't meet, for it's sure Finn will make a paste out of him at once."

"Arrgh! I am Cucullin, I am!" he cried. "And when I see this Finn, I'll flatten him like a pancake!"

Finn whimpered.

"Look, now, you've gone and woken the baby," said Oonagh hastily, beginning to rock the cradle with her foot. "Have you never seen him then, my Finn MacCoul?"

"Hah! 'Tis no wonder I have not – how could I?" answered the giant. "For it's a fact, as everyone knows, he hides from me like a rabbit in a bush."

"Well, when you do see him, and it's sure you will, it will be a black day for you indeed," Oonagh declared. "Why, in all of Ireland, there is none braver or stronger than my Finn."

"Now," said Oonagh, "the wind is blowing through the door. Would you be so kind as to turn the house? Which is what Finn does, of course, when he is here, which as you can see, he is not."

Cucullin was surprised, but he pulled his golden finger three times and went outside. With one great grunt, he picked up the house and turned it around, away from the wind.

Finn groaned and hid deeper under the covers.

"Why, thank you," said Oonagh, when Cucullin returned. "Even though you two may be enemies, I will not be rude. Sit down and have yourself a bite to eat."

She brought him a huge stack of cabbages, a great sack of potatoes, and the sides of three whole cows and five pigs. Cucullin, known to be a glutton as well as a bully, shoved all the food down at once.

"Here then," said Oonagh. "Have some bread."

Cucullin grabbed three loaves and stuffed them into his mouth.

"Aaagh!" he cried, and spat out three teeth. "And what kind of bread is this?"

"Why, it's the only kind Finn ever eats," replied Oonagh.

"Hrrumph," said Cucullin, and shoved in three more loaves. He chomped down and spat out three more teeth.

"Woman!" he cried. "I won't have a tooth left in my head! Why, who eats this devil's bread, hard as a rock?"

"Only Finn himself – and that wee child there in the cradle," said Oonagh.

"Ah, Finn's child will be hungry now, in fact," said Oonagh, and she gave Finn a loaf – of course, one with no iron pot inside. Finn chewed it right up. And then he ate three more.

Cucullin could not believe his eyes. *If this wee lad of Finn's can eat this bread*, he wondered, *then I may not be so sorry to find his father away from home.*

Cucullin walked over and looked in the cradle. "Such a big child he is," he said. "Is he strong?"

Finn sat up in the cradle.

"And are you yourself strong?" he asked Cucullin.

"By the sun and the moon above me!" the giant exclaimed. "Why, such a voice for a lad so young!"

"Well, are you yourself strong?" Finn asked again. "Let me see you crush one of these stones."

Cucullin snorted and picked up one of the great yellow stones. He squeezed and squeezed until he fell down, out of breath, blue in the face, and still the stone had not cracked.

"Ah, you poor creature," said Oonagh. "Giant that you are, you are weak as a bird. Let me show you what the son of Finn MacCoul can do."

Oonagh gave Finn a round of yellow cheese and he squashed it to pieces in a second.

"Oh no!" cried Cucullin, and his knees trembled and knocked. *If this mere child can crush stones*, he decided, *surely then I am no match for the father.*

"I must take my leave now," said Cucullin to Oonagh. "It really is not necessary for me to meet Finn himself, but I would like to look at that young one's teeth to see how he can eat bread made of iron."

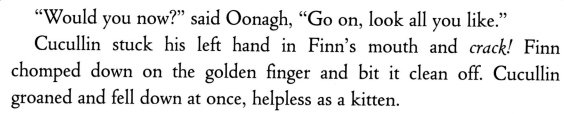

"Would you now?" said Oonagh, "Go on, look all you like."

Cucullin stuck his left hand in Finn's mouth and *crack!* Finn chomped down on the golden finger and bit it clean off. Cucullin groaned and fell down at once, helpless as a kitten.

Finn jumped out of the cradle and gave poor Cucullin a mighty kick. So mighty it was that Cucullin smashed right through the door and rolled down Knockmany Hill, squashing and scattering everything in his path.

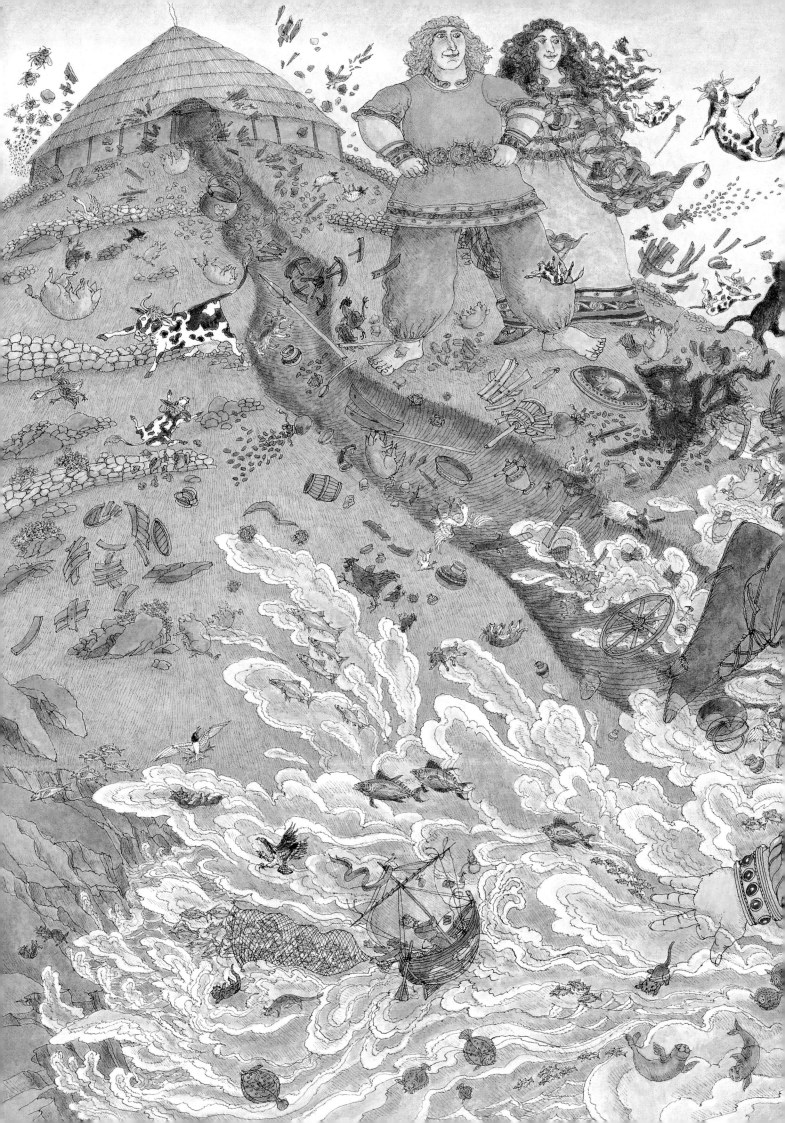

He rolled all the way down to the sea, making such a thunderous splash that the water came half-way back up the hill. To this very day he has never been seen or heard from again.

And so, thanks to Oonagh the fearless, Finn overcame with wit and wisdom that which might never have been done by force.

Finn and Oonagh spent the rest of their days together, both very happy, with the wind always to their backs, and their faces to the sun.

The End

 AFTERWORD

In my version of the story, I have used three basic sources:

Celtic Fairy Tales, by Joseph Jacobs, 1892

Fairy and Folktales of Ireland, edited by W. B. Yeats, 1888 (which includes "A Legend of Knockmany," by William Carlton)

Irish Fairy Tales, by James Stephens, 1920, illustrated by the great Arthur Rackham.

I've tried to combine the most interesting elements of these versions into my account.

The mythical hero Finn MacCoul (in Gaelic spelled *Fionn Mac Cumhal*) appears in a cycle of tales set in the third-century A.D. This particular story takes place in Ulster, the northernmost of the four old kingdoms that make up what we now call Ireland and Northern Ireland.

Finn led the Fianna, or Fenians, great warriors who protected the ancient High Kings. Finn's son Ossian (Oisìn) was a warrior poet and is credited with recording most of Finn's adventures. Finn was descended from the Tuatha De Danann, an early race of giants. He seems to have been the most mortal of the old mythical heroes, considered a thinking man and therefore more susceptible to human foibles.

In Celtic mythology, gods, men and beasts move together across a confusing landscape where magic plays a central role. A belief in faeries and speaking

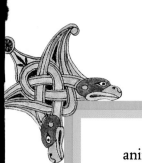

animals flourished in such stories. I have used the old spelling "faery"; the word refers both to the Land of Faery and those who live there.

In this tale, Finn and his giant adversary Cucullin (Cùchulain) collide in a battle of wits presided over and eventually won by Oonagh, Finn's courageous wife, with the help of a bit of magic. This is the only story I found in which Cucullin plays the villain. In all other descriptions he is a great champion of Ulster, even referred to as a Celtic Achilles.

The Giant's Causeway still exists, and the geometrically shaped rocks do look man-made. Formed from volcanic basalt, these boulders are rumoured to have once connected Ireland and Scotland. Similar rock formations are found in nearby Scottish islands.

In the ancient Celtic world, oak groves were sacred. Only the druids (priests) could enter them.

In Celtic societies, women were given fairly equal status with their men. Some became rulers of tribes and even fought in battle.

Celts loved ornament and decoration. Men and women of the noble or warrior class wore extensive jewellery: armbands, bracelets, golden neck torcs, and jewelled broaches. Organic dyes were used in making brightly coloured, patterned clothing.

Houses were made of mud and sticks (wattle and daub), held up by wooden beams and topped with thatched straw roofs. Bread was baked in beehive shaped ovens.

The decorative letters and designs I've used are based on images from the illuminated manuscripts of Celtic monks. I have also incorporated into my pictures some of the animals and birds mentioned in Irish poetry, particularly the epic poems. Even the great Irish elk, now extinct, whose rack of antlers reached fifteen feet, appears in the night scene.

I would be gratified if my narrative and pictures provide readers with some sense of early Celtic life – and, of course, a good story, too.

Robert Byrd

A Note on the Pronunciation of Gaelic Names

FINN MacCOUL (Fionn Mac Cumhal)   Finn Mac-COOL
  (*Finn* means "white" or "fair")

CUCULLIN (Cùchulain)   COO-hullan
  (*Cù* from the word for "hound" – the hound of Cullan)

OONAGH   OOna (the *h* silences the consonant preceding it)

BRAN   Brahn

RÒS DUBH   Rosh-DU

OSSIAN (oisìn)   Uh-SHEEN

FINTAN   FIN-tin

FIANNA   FEE-anna

TUATHA De DANANN   TU-a-ha day DAHN-nun

GAELIC   GAY-lic